DAISY
Yuk!

To Sue Brandon, my fabric guru – K.G.
To Isabel – N.S.

DAISY: YUK!
A RED FOX BOOK 978 1 782 95647 1
First published in Great Britain by The Bodley Head, an imprint of Random House Children's Publishers UK
A Penguin Random House Company

The Bodley Head edition published 2004
Red Fox edition published 2005
This edition published 2016

1 3 5 7 9 10 8 6 4 2

Text copyright © Kes Gray, 2004
Illustrations copyright © Nick Sharratt, 2004

The right of Kes Gray and Nick Sharratt to be identified as the author and illustrator of this work
has been asserted in accordance with the Copyright, Designs and Patents Act 1988.

Penguin Random House is committed to a sustainable future for our business, our readers and our planet.
This book is made from Forest Stewardship Council® certified paper.

Red Fox Books are published by Random House Children's Publishers UK,
61–63 Uxbridge Road, London W5 5SA

www.randomhousechildrens.co.uk www.randomhouse.co.uk

Addresses for companies within The Random House Group Limited can be found at: www.randomhouse.co.uk/offices.htm

THE RANDOM HOUSE GROUP Limited Reg. No. 954009

A CIP catalogue record for this book is available from the British Library.

Printed in China

DAISY
Yuk!

Kes Gray & Nick Sharratt

RED FOX

Daisy didn't do dresses.

"You can't be a bridesmaid if you won't wear a dress," explained her mum.

"Then I won't be a bridesmaid," humphed Daisy.

Daisy's mum put her arm
around Daisy's shoulder.
"If you don't wear a dress to
Auntie Sue and Clive's wedding,
I'll be sad,
Nanny will be sad,
Grampy will be sad,
Clive will be sad,
everyone in the whole
world will be sad,"
exaggerated Daisy's mum.

Daisy unfolded her arms and sighed.
"I'll wear my football kit!" offered Daisy.

"Bridesmaids don't wear
football kits," sighed Daisy's mum.

"Scuba gear looks good!" offered Daisy.

"Or how about a leopard skin suit?"

"We're going to be in a church, Daisy, not a zoo," sighed Daisy's mum.

"At least come and try some dresses on,"
said Auntie Sue.

"Yes," said Daisy's *mum*. "Please come and try some
dresses on. I think *you'd* look lovely in a dress."

Daisy stuck her hands in her pockets and shrugged her shoulders. She didn't do lovely either.

"If I don't like them, I'm not wearing them," she grumbled.

Daisy's mum and Auntie Sue smiled at each other
and rushed Daisy to the wedding dress shop
before she could change her mind.

Daisy tried the first dress on.

It was passion pink satin with rosebuds and frilly bits.

"Yuk," said Daisy.

Daisy tried the second dress on.

It was yellow silk with sequins and soppy gloves.

"Yuk," said Daisy.

Daisy tried the third dress on.

It was blue velvet with bows and puffy sleeves.

"Yuk," said Daisy.

Daisy tried on every bridesmaid dress in the shop.

But the cotton and the tartan and the organza and the chiffon and the lace and the pleats and the petticoats and the ruffles and the sashes and the embroidery and the appliqué and the ribbons and the tiaras and the handbags and the headdresses were all *yuk*.

Yuk!

Yuk!

Daisy's mum looked at Auntie Sue.

Auntie Sue looked at the dress shop owner.

Everyone had run out of ideas.

Except Daisy.

"I'll tell you what," said Daisy. "I will wear a dress if
I can draw it myself."

Daisy's mum raised her eyebrows and looked at Auntie Sue.

"It's a deal," said Auntie Sue.

When Daisy got home, she ran upstairs and closed her bedroom door. She laid out some big pieces of paper on her bedroom floor and tipped the crayons from her pencil case onto her bed.

When Daisy's *mum* came upstairs to call Daisy to dinner, she found a note pinned to Daisy's bedroom door.

When Daisy's *mum* came upstairs with Daisy's pyjamas she found another note pinned to Daisy's door.

"I do hope it isn't a vampire's dress," sighed Daisy's *mum*.

On the day of the wedding, a smiling Auntie Sue arrived at the church, wearing her wedding dress.

It was white satin with sequins
and lacy bows and came with
a rosebud tiara.

Behind Auntie Sue came a smiling Daisy, wearing her bridesmaid's dress.

It was green silk and came with a black ninja headband, *maximum* confetti action belt and hidden extras.

Confety akshun belt

Ninjer hed band

Secrit confety powch

confety

The moment the wedding was over, Daisy reached for her confetti action belt and blammed everybody big time.

She got Auntie Sue down the front of her dress and Uncle Clive down his collar.

She got the Vicar in the ear,

Nanny in the handbag,

and Grampy in the camera.

"How do you like me in a dress?" laughed Daisy, hitting her mum right in the mush with two handfuls.

Daisy's *mum* sighed and began picking bits of confetti out from between her teeth.
"Yuk, Daisy!" she spluttered.

"Yuk, yuk, yuk, yuk, yuk!"